SIX SNOWY SHEEP

For cousin Carol Susie, who is one day older,
despite the snow job, and who makes us
fall down laughing. xoxoxo

—S.G.T & J.R.E.

For Tess
—J. O'B.

Text copyright © 1994 by Judith Ross Enderle and
Stephanie Gordon Tessler
Illustrations copyright © 1994 by John O'Brien

Published by Caroline House
Boyds Mills Press, Inc.
A Highlights Company
815 Church Street
Honesdale, Pennsylvania 18431
Printed in Mexico

First edition, 1994
Book designed by John O'Brien
The text of this book is set in 20-point Goudy.
The illustrations are done in pen and ink,
dyes, and watercolors.
Distributed by St. Martin's Press

10 9 8 7 6 5 4 3 2 1

Publisher Cataloging-in-Publication Data
Enderle, Judith Ross.
    Six snowy sheep / by Judith Ross Enderle and Stephanie Gordon Tessler ;
illustrated by John O'Brien.—1st ed.
[24]p. : col. ill. ; cm.
Summary : Six sheep, one by one, frolic in the snow and five wind up in a
snowbank. The sixth sheep shovels them out.
ISBN 1-56397-138-0
1. Sheep—Fiction—Juvenile literature. 2. Picture books—Juvenile literature.
[1. Sheep—Fiction.] I. Tessler, Stephanie Gordon. II. O'Brien, John, ill.
III. Title.
    [E]—dc20   1994   CIP
Library of Congress Catalog Card Number 93-73307

SIX SNOWY SHEEP

By Judith Ross Enderle and
Stephanie Gordon Tessler

Illustrated by John O'Brien

Boyds Mills Press

Six snowy sheep, snug in woolly warm fleece,
played one wintry Christmas Day.

Soon one snowy sheep, in a daring sheep feat,
sat on his sled.

THEN . . .

Whoosh! He went swooping down the hill and—

Shmoosh! into a snowbank.

Now five snowy sheep, snug in woolly warm fleece, played one wintry Christmas Day.

Soon one snowy sheep, in a daring sheep feat, slipped on his skates.

THEN . . .

Whoops! He went skittering across the pond and—
Shmoosh! into a snowbank.

Now four snowy sheep, snug in woolly warm fleece,
played one wintry Christmas Day.

Soon one snowy sheep, in a daring sheep feat,
strapped on his skis.

THEN . . .

Swoosh! He went schussing down the slope and—

Shmoosh! into a snowbank.

Now three snowy sheep, snug in woolly warm fleece,
played one wintry Christmas Day.

Soon one snowy sheep, in a daring sheep feat, stepped into his snowshoes.

THEN . . .

Squoosh! He went stomping through the woods and—
Shmoosh! into a snowbank.

Now two snowy sheep, snug in woolly warm fleece, played one wintry Christmas Day.

Soon one snowy sheep, in a daring sheep feat, settled in his saucer.

THEN . . .

Whoa! He went swirling down the slope and—
Shmoosh! into a snowbank.

Now one snowy sheep, snug in woolly warm fleece, played one wintry Christmas Day.

And he shoveled and shoveled and shoveled and shoveled and finally found . . .

five shaky, shivery, soggy sheep.

THEN . . .

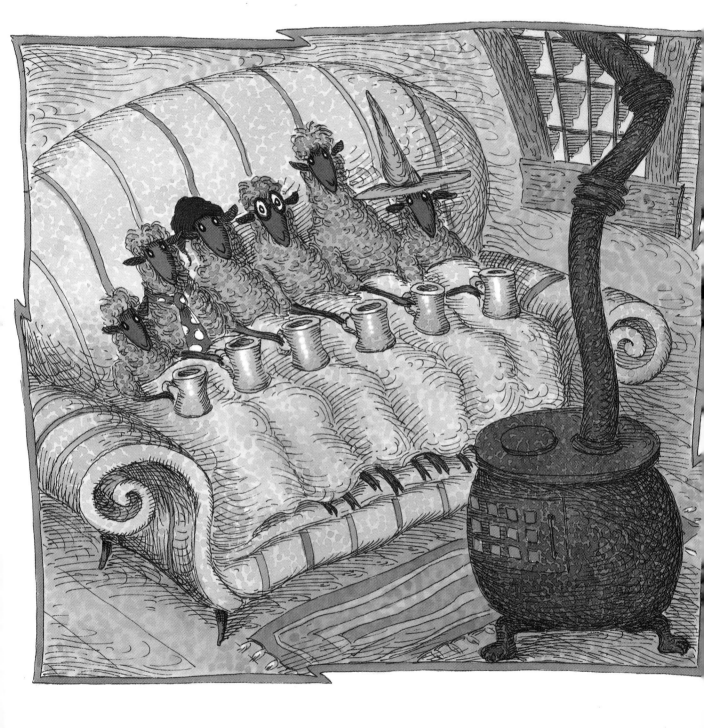